HELLO, I'M THEA!

I'm *Geronimo Stilton*'s sister. As I'm sure you know from my brother's bestselling novels, I'm a special correspondent for *The Rodent's Gazette*, Mouse Island's most famous newspaper. Unlike my 'fraidy mouse brother, I absolutely adore traveling, having adventures, and meeting rodents from all around the world!

The adventure I want to tell you about takes place at Mouseford Academy, the school I went to when I was a young mouseling. I had such a great experience there as a student that I came back to teach a journalism class.

When I returned as a grown mouse, I met five really special students: Colette, Nicky, Pamela, Paulina, and Violet. You could hardly imagine five more different mouselings, but they became great friends right away. And they liked me so much that they decided to name their group after me: the Thea Sisters! I was so touched by that, I decided to write about their adventures. So turn the page to discover the first fabumouse adventure of the

THEA SISTERS!

Name: Nicky
Nickname: Nic
Home: Australia
Secret ambition: Wants to be an ecologist.
Loves: Open spaces and nature.
Strengths: She is always in a good mood, as long as she's outdoors!

Weaknesses: She can't sit still!

Secret: Nicky is claustrophobic — she can't stand being in small, tight places.

Nicky

COLETTE

Name: Colette

Nickname: It's Colette, please. (She can't stand nicknames.)

Home: France

Secret ambition: Colette is very particular about her appearance. She wants to be a fashion writer.

Loves: The color pink.

Strengths: She's energetic and full of great ideas.

Weaknesses: She's always late!

Secret: To relax, there's nothing Colette likes more than a manicure and pedicure.

Colette

VIOLET

Name: Violet

Nickname: Vi

Home: China

Secret ambition: Wants to become a great violinist.

Loves: Books! She is a real intellectual, just like my brother, Geronimo.

Strengths: She's detail-oriented and always open to new things.

Weaknesses: She is a bit sensitive and can't stand being teased. And if she doesn't get enough sleep, she can be a real grouch!

Secret: She likes to unwind by listening to classical music and drinking green tea.

Violet

Name: Paulina

Nickname: Polly

Home: Peru

Secret ambition: Wants to be a scientist.

Loves: Traveling and meeting people from all over the world. She is also very close to her sister, Maria.

Strengths: Loves helping other rodents.

Weaknesses: She's shy and can be a bit clumsy.

Secret: She is a computer genius!

PAULINA

PAULINA

Name: Pamela
Nickname: Pam
Home: Tanzania
Secret ambition: Wants to become a sports journalist or a car mechanic.
Loves: Pizza, pizza, and more pizza! She'd eat pizza for breakfast if she could.
Strengths: She is a peacemaker. She can't stand arguments.
Weaknesses: She is very impulsive.
Secret: Give her a screwdriver and any mechanical problem will be solved!

Pamela

Geronimo Stilton

Thea Stilton
AND THE
DRAGON'S CODE

Scholastic Inc.

New York   Toronto   London   Auckland   Sydney
Mexico City   New Delhi   Hong Kong   Buenos Aires

ISBN-13: 978-0-545-10367-1
ISBN-10: 0-545-10367-3

Text by Thea Stilton, with assistance from Piccolo Tao
Original title *Il Codice del Drago*
Cover by Flavio Ferron and Giuseppe Facciotto
Illustrations by Fabio Bono, Federica Salfo, Giada Perissinotto, Giorgio Di Vita, Ida Maria Beretta, Luca Usai, Manuela Razzi, Marco Failla, Marco Gervasio, Marco Meloni, Marco Palazzi, Massimo Asaro, Rafaella Seccia, and Sergio Cabella

Graphics by Merenguita Gingermouse and Superpao, with assistance from Michela Battaglin

Special thanks to Beth Dunfey
Interior design by Kay Petronio

12 11 10 9 8 7 6 5   9 10 11 12 13 14/0

Printed in the U.S.A.
First printing, April 2009

A MYSTERIOUS INVITATION

It all started one September evening. I was working late at *The Rodent's Gazette*, the newspaper run by my brother, *Geronimo Stilton*.

I had just turned in my last article — an investigation into a case of smuggled cheese. I couldn't wait to get home to take a NICE RELAXING BATH.

THEA STILTON

I scampered home as fast as my tired paws could take me. As I

Help the members of the Thea Sisters solve the mystery! When you see this magnifying glass, pay attention: It means there's an important clue on that page.

opened the door to my apartment building, I caught a glimpse of a rodent dressed as a postmouse. He stared at me suspiciously.

"THEA STILTON?" he squeaked.

"YES, that's me," I answered.

"Thea Stilton, the famouse sister of the really FAMOUSE Geronimo Stilton?" he asked.

"YES, I'm Thea," I responded impatiently. Was my brother really more famouse than me? I'd never really thought about it before.

"THEA STILTON, the famouse sister of the really famouse *Geronimo Stilton*, the publisher and editor in chief of *The Rodent's Gazette*, the most famouse newspaper on Mouse Island?" he asked.

"YES, YES, and YEEEEEEEES!" I shouted.

He jumped back a step. "Rat-munching rattlesnakes, mind your manners, please! I just wanted to be sure. I have a very important letter for you. Blue envelope, parchment paper, red wax seal — this is *fancy stuff*!"

He was right. The letter really *did* look **important**. But who was it from?

Who? Who?? Who???

"Do you have any idea how long I've been WAITING for you?" the postmouse squeaked. He seemed a little put out. "I suppose I could have put the letter in the mailbox, but what if someone came along and stole it?"

This postmouse was taking his responsibilities a little too seriously. He was starting to make me **NERVOUS**. So I grabbed the letter and headed up to my mouse hole.

"Thanks a million!" I told him as I scurried up the stairs. "It was really nice of you to wait for me."

MOUSEFORD ACADEMY

A DRAGON WITH AN "m" IN ITS CLAWS

By this time, *curiosity* was burning me up. Before I ripped open the letter, I noticed that the red wax seal was marked with a dragon holding the letter **M** in its claws.

I knew the symbol well: It was the **MOUSEFORD ACADEMY** seal!

Being accepted as a student at Mouseford Academy is a huge intellectual achievement. And teaching there is an honor. Only the best and **brightest** mice on all of Mouse Island study and teach at Mouseford Academy.

So why were they contacting *me*?

My tail started *twitching* nervously. I broke the seal, opened the envelope, and . . .

WOW!

DOUBLE WOW!

TRIPLE WOW WITH WHIPPED CHEESE AND A CHERRY ON TOP

It was for me, THEA STILTON. I had received an invitation to teach a course in **ADVENTURE JOURNALISM** to a group of specially chosen **STUDENTS** at Mouseford Academy!

I was happy. I was excited. I was thrilled from the tips of my whiskers to the tip of my tail!

Years ago, back when I was just a mouseling, I had been CHOSEN to attend

DID YOU KNOW?

The oldest types of **seals** were made by sealing a rolled-up document with wax. Then whoever had written the message would press his crest into the wax when it was still soft. That way, the intended recipient would know the document had arrived without being opened.

Today, seals are also used for everyday purposes. For example, jars of food are sealed with a strip of plastic that joins the jar to the lid. If the plastic strip has remained intact, we can be sure the jar has never been opened!

Mouseford Academy. And now they were choosing me again — to teach there!

I felt a tingling sensation in my whiskers. I always get that feeling at the beginning of a **new adventure**.

I couldn't wait for my adventure to begin!

Congratulations!

Bravo!

Thank you, Professor!

A NIGHT FULL OF STARS AND WISHES

I checked the weather forecast, because the only way to get to MOUSEFORD ACADEMY is by SEA. It was built more than a thousand years ago on WHALE ISLAND, a triangle of rocks and woods southwest of Mouse Island. Fortunately, I am an excellent sailor, if I do squeak so myself!

The forecast wasn't good. The weather would hold for one day — two at the most — with a strong southerly WIND, which was ideal for sailing toward my destination. After that, it looked like there were going to be storms with gusts of wind from the North.

WHALE ISLAND

I did some quick thinking. It was four days until my first class. In theory, I could take my time. But that north wind might blow me off course, and I absolutely hate to be late.

So I made my decision: I would set off **at once**. So much for my nice, relaxing bath! When you live the life of a special correspondent, you have to make snap decisions. And you get used to giving up little LUXURIES like baths, clean clothes, cheese, and sleep!

I rushed over to my closet and started

Evening dress

Red sweater

Hiking boots

Raincoat

packing. First I put the things I would need immediately in my backpack: my camera and laptop, a *lavender* dress for important evenings out, a **RED** sweater and hiking boots for outdoor trips, a raincoat for the crossing, and a **blue** tracksuit for everyday wear.

Then I pulled out my trunk and filled it to the brim with other things I'd need for my stay at Mouseford Academy: my *favorite* books on journalism, samples of my own past work in *The Rodent's Gazette*, more clothes, shoes, and pictures of my family.

Tracksuit

Once I was all packed, I took a quick shower and dressed in my **warmest** clothes. Then I hailed a taxi and headed for New Mouse City Harbor.

By midnight, I had already put out to sea. (I love to sail and I have my own catamaran.) What a fabumouse evening to be on the ocean! The night **STARS** shone like diamonds. Every now and then, a shooting star would illuminate the **DARKNESS**. I made so many wishes that night!

It was a magical evening. But then **HE** arrived.

THE CATAMARAN

A **catamaran** is a sailboat with two hulls that are joined together. Its name comes from the Tamil words *kattu*, which means "to tie," and *maram*, which means "wood." The biggest catamaran ever built is 145 feet long and 54.5 feet wide!

11

HOW'D YOU GET YOUR LICENSE?

Thanks to a strong southern wind, I was *flying* across the water! At dawn, I caught a glimpse of **WHALE ISLAND**. I spotted a **blue** whale passing my catamaran, so I slowed down to study it more closely.

I was busy admiring my new friend, when I noticed a long line of **WHITE FOAM** rise up on the horizon.

I pulled out my binoculars to get a closer look. The white foam was moving.

FAST!

VERY FAST!!

REALLY, REALLY FAST!!!

Greasy cat guts!

The foam was coming from a HYDROPLANE, a high-powered seaplane fitted with enormous floats that allow it to land on and take off from water. And that hydroplane was coming toward me at an incredible speed.

BLUE WHALES

The **blue whale** is the largest animal to have ever lived on Earth — it's even bigger than the biggest dinosaurs! A typical adult is 90 to 100 feet long and can weigh more than 100 tons.

I made a few sharp turns and managed to avoid being **HIT**. The hydroplane shot past on the starboard side (that is, to the right), missing me by a whisker.

But I wasn't completely safe. As it whizzed by, the hydroplane generated a huge wave that completely engulfed me.

SPLASSSH!!!!!

I was soaked to the fur!

And even worse, a baby octopus had landed on my snout! Its **tentacles** were wrapped around my ears.

Once I'd untangled myself, I shouted, **"HOW'D YOU GET YOUR LICENSE?!"**

But the hydroplane was already too far away for its captain to hear me. He was going in the direction of Whale Island, too. I couldn't wait to **catch up** with that captain so I could give him a piece of my mind!

VINCE GUYMOUSE

I was still fuming as I brought my catamaran into the harbor at Whale Island. And there he was — the captain of the hydroplane!

He was sitting on the pier next to his hydroplane, acting like a big rat on campus with every rodent who passed.

"Did you see my fabumouse docking maneuver? Not to toot my own horn, but I'm one of the **best** captains on the Sea of Mice. Hmm, make that *the* best!"

Can you believe his nerve?

That was when he noticed me standing there. He must have thought I was pretty (I often have that effect on male mice), because he strode up, took my paw, and kissed it. "Allow me to introduce myself. My name

is **VINCE GUYMOUSE**. It is a great, great pleasure to meet you."

I yanked my paw away. "*Oh, the pleasure is all mine!*" I replied with a glare.

Guymouse was so surprised, he almost jumped out of his fur. He stepped back, tripping over his two hind paws.

I took advantage of his confusion by

"Oh, the pleasure is all mine!"

STICKING a tangled mass of stinky *algae* on his snout.

"*Captain? You?* My catamaran was standing still, and you almost crashed into me!"

I was so agitated, my tail was twitching. I couldn't seem to stop it. That's when I heard a peculiar sound, like a clap.

Then another. Clap-clap.
Clap-clap-clap-clap-clap.

Someone was applauding me!

THE RULES OF THE SEA

Boats that are more difficult to maneuver have the **right of way**. That means that sailboats have the right of way over motorboats.

A good captain always pays close attention to the boats in the area, even when his or her boat has the right of way. The other boat may be experiencing difficulties in maneuvering, or maybe its captain is distracted. And, of course, boats that aren't moving must be avoided at all costs!

FIVE BRIGHT-LOOKING MOUSELINGS

Standing behind me on the dock were five *bright-looking* mouselings. Four were clapping for me while the fifth, who had *beautiful* almond-shaped eyes and long **black** hair, stood a little to the side.

Meanwhile, Vince Guymouse was still sitting on the dock, trying to *pick* the bits of algae out of his whiskers.

"Well done!" said the first mouseling, who had **DARK FUR** and thick, curly hair. "That rodent was really cheesing me off!"

The second mouse, with a REALLY LOOOOOOOOOONG braid, darted forward to explain. "*Pamela* and I couldn't take another minute of his bragging." Then she looked at me shyly and said, "You must be Thea Stilton."

"THEA STILTON?" said the third mouseling, who was wearing an enormouse cowboy hat. "Wow! Would you be so kind as to give me your autograph?"

"Sure," I replied laughing. "But please, let's not be so formal."

The second mouseling piped up again. "That's Nicky and I'm PAULINA. Those two over there are Colette and Violet." She shook my paw.

Colette had blond fur and was dressed in pink from snout to tail. As she spoke, she paused every now and then to blow on her hot-pink nail polish. "You see, we were on board . . . PUFF . . . the plane with him. It was an awful journey . . . PUFF . . . UP and DOWN all the time . . . PUFF. I put on my lipstick and it smudged all over my snout . . . PUFF. So I waited until we were back on dry land before freshening up my nail polish."

Nicky nodded. "What a trip! It was a wild ride. Worse than riding on a cat with fleas!"

"Excuse me for interrupting," said **Violet**,

COLETTE

PAMELA

PAULINA

NICKY

VIOLET

Worse than riding on a cat with fleas! Worse than riding on a cat with fleas!

the mouseling with black hair and almond-shaped eyes. "But what do you think we should do about **him**?"

She meant Vince Guymouse, of course. I'd almost forgotten all about him.

Vince Guymouse

MOUSEY SIGHS

Paulina, the mouseling with the long braid, came over to look at Guymouse.

"Yuck! The smell must be getting to him!" she said, holding her nose. The algae really *did* let off quite a **stench**.

Vince Guymouse was sitting on the ground, looking confused.

"To say that something **stinks** or **smells nice** depends on your point of view, doesn't it, Ms. Stilton?" asked Violet. She giggled and put a paw in front of her nose. "I bet we'll learn about that in your journalism class." Then she pointed to the algae. "But I think we can objectively observe that flies adore this *algae* here."

Colette took a small bottle filled with *pink* liquid out of her *pink* bag. "**Poor thing!** He probably has a very delicate sense of smell. Let me help him."

She poured two *pink* drops onto a *pink* pawkerchief and waved it under his snout. The flies flew away in a hurry. As for Vince, he twitched his whiskers, then let out a LONG SIGH. He rubbed his eyes and looked around.

Colette stuck the cloth under his snout again. Slowly, he got back on his paws and looked around.

"That's some perfume you have there," I told Colette. "What is the name?"

"**CAPTAIN VINCE GUYMOUSE**," mumbled the befuddled captain.

"Not **your** name!" I said. "The name of the perfume."

Colette winked at me. "The perfume is called *Mousey Sighs*."

"Oh, yes, I've heard of it," I said, smiling. "A very appropriate name, too!"

Everyone burst out *laughing*. I had a good feeling about these mouselings. I could just tell we were going to hit it off. And that made me remember how EXCITED I was about teaching at Mouseford! If all my students were like these five, it was sure to be an **AMAZING** experience.

There was just one thing that wasn't **quite right**. Ever since I'd landed, I felt a kind of nervous tingling in my whiskers, like someone was watching us. But who?

PERFUME

The oldest technique used for making perfume is **distillation.** The distillation process is simple: Boil some water along with flowers, fruit, or sweet-smelling wood until it turns into steam. The steam "captures" the smells, and turns into a perfumed liquid when cooled. It might sound easy, but making perfume isn't something you should try at home. It requires special equipment and is best left to the professionals!

ONE MORE, NOT ONE LESS!

I turned in the direction of MOUSEFORD CASTLE. What a glorious sight! As I gazed at the tallest tower, I glimpsed the **shadow** of someone behind the arched windows. It was probably another teacher preparing for the semester to begin.

I said good-bye to the five mouselings, gathered up my belongings, and set off along the path to the school.

What a day! The SUN was shining, and walking toward campus brought back so many memories.

I was getting closer to the academy now. I could already read the school's motto on the plaque at the main entrance:

ONE MORE, NOT ONE LESS!

It meant "one more crossing the threshold of knowledge, never one less!" It was one of the many things about Mouseford that I admired.

As I approached the school gates, I heard someone yell, "WHERE DO YOU THINK YOU'RE GOING?"

That high, **screechy** squeak reminded me of someone. I looked over to see a stout figure in blue overalls emerge from the courtyard's shadows.

"I've just finished cleaning that floor," he continued. "So don't go getting dirty pawprints all over it!"

Why, yes! That's who he reminded me of! He sounded just like the **postmouse** who had delivered my invitation to teach at Mouseford! He had the same *high-pitched* squeak.

"Excuse me," I interrupted. "Do you have a brother, by any chance?"

"**NO**, I don't," he squeaked huffily. "Now off with you! And wipe your paws on the mat before entering!"

This rodent was crabbier than the cats in the New Mouse City Zoo, but it wasn't my job to teach him good manners. So I nodded and continued on my way, daydreaming about my student days.

THE HONOR IS ALL MINE!

I stepped into the entrance hall and found myself at the foot of a long staircase. The walls all around me were papered with **ANCIENT MAPS** of the world. I smiled. How well I remembered scampering up and down these stairs as a young mouseling! I think the maps had inspired my love of travel and adventure.

Professor Octavius de Mousus, the headmaster of Mouseford Academy, came out of his office to welcome me.

Professor Octavius de Mousus

"My dear Ms. Stilton, it is an honor to see you again," he said, extending his paw.

"The honor is all mine," I replied.

"No," he insisted, gazing at me seriously. "The honor is *mine*."

We looked each other right in the eye as if daring the other to blink.

One second passed . . .

Two seconds passed . . .

Three seconds passed . . .

Then we both **burst out** laughing!

The headmaster spread his arms out wide. "Dearest Thea, what an immense *pleasure* it is to see you again!"

We hugged each other affectionately, like old friends. Well, that was what we were now: **FRIENDS!** Of course, it hadn't always been that way. When I was a student and he was *headmaster*, I was a little afraid of

him. But as I GREW UP,
I came to understand
that even the strictest
of rodents can have a
heart as soft as
cheese spread!

The headmaster
invited me into his
study. It was exactly
as I remembered it:
the well-worn sofa and
matching chairs; the fireplace, complete with
a portrait of Mouseford's founder, the scholar
Augustus Mouseford; the bookshelves
crowded with **OLD BOOKS**; and the
immense wooden desk, always immaculately
tidy, with a quill pen and an old-fashioned
inkwell.

"Ah, Thea, I remember so clearly

Orazio Wonderrat

Thea Stilton

Bartholomew Sparkle

what you were like as a young student," he said. "You were always a bit **RECKLESS**!" He pointed a paw at my photograph on the wall. "But even then, your intelligence put you snout and shoulders above the pack!"

I went **a bit red**. (The *headmaster* is the only person in the world who can embarrass me!) It meant so much to hear him squeak those words. And I was proud to see my photo up there on the wall along with those of Mouseford's *finest*!

The headmaster offered me tea and *sugared* cheddar biscuits. As we talked, I learned that I was the FIRST of the teachers to arrive: Professor Wonderrat and Bartholomew Sparkle were yet to come.

Professor de Mousus couldn't wait for me to meet Professor Sparkle. "He earned his degree last year, but has already proved to be an *excellent* scholar," the headmaster told me.

I lingered for a few minutes and **nibbled** away at the headmaster's snacks. Then we heard some voices in the distance. I glanced out the study window and spotted the five mouselings I had met earlier walking along the path.

TWO RATHER BIZARRE MICE

Professor de Mousus kindly offered to show me my room. Together we set off toward the stairway that led down to the ground floor.

Suddenly . . . *baaam!*

The door to the library burst open. From inside, we could hear *loud thuds* and *crashes*. Curious, I peered in.

There on the floor, wedged behind a stepladder and buried beneath piles of . . .

. . . was a long, thin rodent with thick spectacles and an untidy mop of hair.

I rushed over to help him.

"*Squeak!*" he sobbed. "E-everything's OK . . . ouch!"

I could tell he was trying to sound tough, but it wasn't working.

The *headmaster* was a little irked. "Moldy mozzarella! Mr. Ratson, may I ask what you think you're doing?"

The tall, thin mouse apologized: "I-I w-was trying to get a book from the **top** shelf."

As he spoke, he moved aside a volume called *A History of Mouseford Castle*, pushed away a **HUGE** book called *The Complete Manual of Mysterious Ancient Symbols*, and

pulled out a slim volume that had **BOOBY TRAPS: A BEGINNER'S GUIDE** printed on the front cover. "Aha! Here it is!"

"Ms. Stilton, allow me to introduce you to **HANS RATSON**, who is enrolled in the journalism course. He's been here just a few days," the headmaster explained.

"That's right, ahem, hello, Ms. Stilton,"

Hans Ratson?

Clue

said Hans, **blushing** nervously.

What a strange mouse! I don't know why, but he looked a little **familiar**.

I was trying to remember where I'd seen him before when the mouse who had blocked my entrance to the castle appeared.

"**OH, GOOD WORK!**" he said sarcastically to Hans. "I just organized these shelves, and now look what you've done!"

I took the headmaster aside for a moment.

"The handymouse has the same voice as the postmouse I met on New Mouse Island!" I whispered to him.

Professor de Mousus smiled. "That was his brother, **Mercury**, the island postmouse. I asked him to send you your invitation, but

Where have we already seen Hans Ratson? Was it in the headmaster's study?

The Whale Family

1. Devon Whale, the father, a famouse fishermouse.

2. Josephine Whale, the mother, a farmer.

3. Boomer Whale, handymouse at Mouseford Academy.

4. Midge Whale, cook at Mouseford Academy.

5. Mercury Whale, the postmouse and messenger.

6. Oilskin Whale, also known as Smudge, runs the Ancient Cheddar Shop in the village.

7. Leopold Whale, a fishermouse.

8. Michael Whale, left Whale Island at a young age and was never seen again.

The Squid Family

Toady Squid, the mother, a dressmaker (and sister of Devon Whale's grandfather's uncle).

Neptune Squid, the father, a builder (and nephew of Josephine Whale's cousin six times removed).

Mary Squid, a great ballerina who looks after (and breeds) donkeys.

Sardinia Squid, a fishermouse.

Chamomile Squid is usually asleep (and when she's awake, she gets into trouble).

Lavendar Squid runs the local beauty shop with her sister Chamomile.

Francesca-Antonia Squid, also known as Chip-Chop, is a judo champion.

Paulie Squid, also known as Octomouse, is a famouse musclemouse who wouldn't hurt a fly!

he preferred to deliver it in person. Isn't that right, **Boomer**?"

Boomer shot me a dirty look but kept quiet.

"But you lied to me!" I exclaimed. "I asked you if you had a brother, and you said no!"

"You asked me if I had *a* brother, Boomer said huffily. "Well, I don't have a brother, I've got **FOUR**! Ask precise questions if you want precise answers. Now, if you'll excuse me, I have to get back to work!"

HANS RATSON offered to give him a paw.

The more I stared at Hans Ratson, the more certain I became that I'd seen him before!

BUT WHERE?

A LITTLE SQUABBLE

The headmaster took me for a **STROLL** around the grounds. *Nicky*, the student with the cowboy hat, was sitting outside on the grass. She seemed to have beaten the rest of the mouselings to the **CASTLE**. She took off her hat and waved.

The four other mouselings (along with a soggy-looking Vince Guymouse) were still heading up the path to the school. *Pamela* was eating a cheese stick. She was carrying a colorful pawbag and pulling a red suitcase behind her.

PAULINA was next to her, drinking in the sights and sounds of the academy. She had her camera out and photos and observing everything with an attentive eye. She was carrying a backpack, and a laptop case was slung over her shoulder.

Violet strolled along, carrying a violin case and a huge bag over her shoulder. In her paws, she held a red wooden box decorated in gold. You could see that she was very attached to it by the careful way she held it out in front of her.

The last mouseling was Colette, who was scampering along with a tiny pink shoulder bag.

Behind her, bringing up the rear, was VINCE GUYMOUSE. He looked like he was about to collapse under the weight of all the stuff he was carrying — a mountain of bags of all shapes and sizes:

a pink trunk,

a huge pink suitcase,

two pink-and-white-striped hatboxes,

a pale pink overnight bag,

a pink backpack,

a bright pink umbrella,

a pink POLKA-DOTTED shopping bag, and

a pink bottle of mineral water.

They were just a few things that belonged to Colette!

"You're taking advantage of him," said Violet, shaking her snout.

"Well, he offered," Colette answered. "I didn't ask him to do anything!"

"Maybe, but it still doesn't seem right," Violet replied.

"Why?" asked Colette. "Perhaps *you* wanted to carry them for me?"

At this point, Pamela interrupted, "All right! Calm down!"

PAULINA stepped in. "Pam's right," she said. "We all need to relax before a fight breaks out."

Violet shrugged. "I'm not trying to start a fight. I'm just pointing out that it's not polite to — "

"So kind of you, Your Majesty!" snapped Colette.

Pamela tried again. "Come on, *be good!*" she said, smiling. "Look! We're here at last! And Vince has to head back to Mouse Island now, right?"

PAULINA looked up at the sky and shook her snout. "I don't know about that. Look at that falcon up there — it just changed direction! First it had the SOUTHERN wind behind it, and now the wind is coming from the NORTH."

"So what?" asked Colette.

"PAULINA is quite right," I added. "That means the weather is changing! Vince's hydroplane won't be able to take off. When the WIND comes from a northerly direction, it means a storm is going to hit WHALE ISLAND."

PEREGRINE FALCONS

The **peregrine falcon** is a real acrobat! During courtship displays, male and female falcons carry out very complicated movements: bowing, scraping, and exchanging their captured prey. When diving, they can reach speeds of 200 miles per hour!

CHIRP-CHIRP-CHIRP . . . EEK!

The mouselings introduced themselves to Professor de Mousus, and he invited them into his study to discuss their plans for the term. Nicky and I went down to give VINCE a paw with the bags. We were just in time, too! He was about to collapse in a *pool of sweat*. He looked as PALE as a piece of freshly sliced mozzarella.

I offered him a glass of water, then another, then **another**, then **another**.

Before he left, he shot a LONGING look in *Colette*'s direction. Her perfume really had done the trick!

I said good-bye to everyone and went off to take a shower. Professor

de Mousus had pointed me in the direction of my room, so I headed that way and soon found myself in a small but cozy space.

After I'd bathed, I snuggled into my nice comfy bed and closed my eyes for a quick nap. As I lay in bed, dozing, I heard the mouselings exploring their rooms, which were right next door to mine.

Nicky must have grabbed Pamela's bag and thrown it to her: "Catch!"

"Thanks," said Pamela.

"Whose is this?" asked Nicky.

"Oh, that's mine," said Violet quickly. They must have been talking about her fancy red box. "I'll take that."

I could hear pawsteps SCAMPERING to and fro around the rooms. I heard someone say, "This is fabumouse!

TRADITIONS AND HABITS

In Asia, the **cricket** has always been considered good company, as they are said to bring good luck. People in China, Japan, and other parts of Asia have kept pet crickets for hundreds of years.

I can't believe I'm really here at last! Look at the view!"

Then I heard Pamela's voice.

"We've got a problem," she said. "The rooms all contain two beds, and there are five of us. One of us will have to sleep **ALONE**."

"If you don't mind, I want to be with Nicky," said Paulina politely. "We've got lots of things to talk about."

Colette sounded happy to be settling in. "That's fine with me," she said.

"I know!" said Pamela. "We can get a bed from another room and make an apartment for three!"

"That's a great idea!" Nicky agreed. "I'll help you."

"I think it's a good idea, too, but I can't come with you right now," Violet said. "I have to give Frilly something to eat."

"Who's Frilly?" Paulina asked.

I heard a chirp-chirping sound.

"Eeeek!" Pamela squeaked. "What *is* that?"

"It's a cricket!" said Violet. She sounded a little defensive. "And it's my pet. Frilly lives in this little pumpkin."

"Cricket, grasshopper, cockroach . . . they're all the same!" cried Pamela. "They all make me break out in hives!"

Violet sighed so loudly I could hear it right through the wall.

Help!

MOUSEFORD ACADEMY

RULES AND REGULATIONS

1. Mouseford is a place of study. Students are asked to show consideration for their classmates' study habits and conduct themselves with dignity.

2. Mouseford is an ancient place. Students must respect their surroundings. Graffiti and any kind of vandalism are strictly forbidden.

3. Mouseford Library is open to all students. Books must be treated with care and put back on the shelves where they were found.

4. All students are responsible for keeping their rooms clean and tidy.

5. Meals are served according to the schedule posted in the dining hall. The dining hall is for students and teachers alike. Students will be asked to take turns helping out in the kitchen.

6. Mouseford is a place where rodents from different places come together. Here we respect all kinds of traditions from around the world.

7. Students are asked to remain in their rooms at night. No one may leave Mouseford after sunset without permission from the headmaster.

8. The students and teachers at Mouseford are guests of Whale Island. The beliefs and culture of the island's residents must be respected.

9. Whale Island and the sea around it are a protected national park. Everyone is invited to respect nature in all its forms and appearances.

10. The cellars of Mouseford Castle and the area to the north of Whale Island are out of bounds to all students.

HEADMASTER
Octavius de Mousus

OUR STUDENTS   *OUR DORM ROOMS*

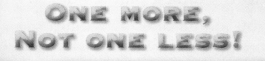

THUNDER AND LIGHTNING

I was sleeping *peacefully* when a window-rattling thunderbolt woke me.

Moldy mozzarella! The weather had changed!

I sat up and looked out the window. The sky was so dark it was practically black. Every so often, it was illuminated by lightning. Thunder rumbled menacingly in the distance. It sounded like the growl of a hungry cat's **BELLY**.

And speaking of hunger, it was dinnertime, according to my clock. I jumped out of bed and got dressed.

As I scurried along the corridors on my way to the dining hall, I noticed the lamps gave off a kind of shaky light.

I then noticed two shadows on the floor. It turned out to be two of my new students.

"*Hello, Ms. Stilton!*"

It was Nicky and Paulina. Paulina *smiled*. "I'm so glad we scampered into you," she said. "I think we're lost!"

"No worries," I replied. "This place is like a **maze**, but you'll get the hang of it. In fact, I think I remember a shortcut to the dining hall. Follow me!"

We veered right and went d o w n a looooooong, winding flight of stairs. AT LAST, WE CAME ACROSS A TINY DOOR.

"Inside-out kangaroo pockets!" exclaimed Nicky. "This isn't the dining hall."

It was a storeroom, filled to the ceiling with strange objects covered in white sheets. A large, sheet-covered shape loomed in front of us. What was it?

I stepped in front of Paulina and whipped off the sheet.

"It's a DRAGON carved out of wood!" Paulina exclaimed.

We gazed at it for a moment. Suddenly, a high-pitched squeak broke the silence.

"What are you

DRAGONS

According to legend, the **dragon** was a symbol of strength. The Vikings carved their longboats with dragons, and medieval knights had them painted on their shields and flags. In the East, however, the dragon represents the rising sun. It is considered a symbol of good luck.

doing here!? You'll **LOSE** your *fur* if you keep sticking your *snouts* where you're not allowed!"

It was *him* again: **Boomer Whale**. He really was a most unpleasant rodent.

I could tell Paulina and Nicky were mortified at being scolded.

As for myself, I was **disgusted** with Boomer's behavior. Yelling was no way to talk to students or a visiting teacher.

Boomer showed us the right way to the dining room.

Boomer Whale

But as I sat down to eat, I realized something hadn't been quite right in that storeroom. It was almost as if there had been something — or some*one* — else there. But what or who had it been?

Someone is hidden in this room.
Can you see him?

IS EVERYTHING OK?

"Gulp it all down or there'll be no dessert!" a voice squeaked **shrilly**.

Guess who was serving dinner at the tables. It was **Midge Whale**, the sister of the postmouse and the handymouse! She never stopped squeaking, not for a moment!

"This **cheddar cheese macaroni** is good, isn't it?" she said. "It's a secret recipe!"

Colette, Paulina, Nicky, Pamela, and **HANS RATSON** (who had turned up out of breath at the last moment) were all sitting at the same table.

Violet sat alone and hardly touched her food. She looked a little lonely. But luckily, Midge seemed to have

Clue

Why did Hans Ratson turn up out of breath at the last moment?

taken a liking to her cricket.

"Isn't he gorgeous?" Midge cooed. "Look how he's munching on the lettuce! He's enjoying EVERY LAST BITE!"

I sat down at the table with my friend the *headmaster* and asked him about the shortcut gone wrong. He explained that we must have taken the stairway that leads to the cellars beneath the castle, an area that is strictly OFF-LIMITS to students.

I took full responsibility for what had happened and told him about Boomer's strange threat: *"You'll lose your* **fur** *if you keep sticking your snouts where you're not* **ALLOWED**!"

The headmaster sighed.

Midge Whale

"Boomer is very superstitious. *Legend* has it that some rodents have disappeared in the cellars. But of course I don't believe it."

At the other table, Hans Ratson and the four mouselings were busy chatting.

Nicky and Paulina were talking about the environment. They belonged to an ecology movement called Green Mice.

Violet had pulled out a book. She reminded me a little bit of my brother, Geronimo. He's quite the bookmouse.

Is everything OK?

I got up and went to Violet's table. "He's a lovely cricket. What's his name?" I asked.

"*Frilly*," she replied without looking up.

"Is everything OK?" I asked.

She SHOOK her snout.

I smiled. "Violet, you should try making friends with the other students. It's great to get to know different mice and share different points of view!"

Before **Violet** could reply, Hans Ratson stood up and yawned. "I'm so tired! It's time for bed."

YAWN!

"Whatever you do, *don't* go scampering around at night!" **Midge** burst out. "You'll lose your fur

69

if you stick your snout where you're not allowed!"

These Whale characters were really rather strange! Why were they so worried about the students wandering around the castle at night?

I WAS STARTING TO THINK THEY HAD SOMETHING TO HIDE.

ISN'T IT ABOUT TIME YOU PUT TWO AND TWO TOGETHER?

- Ever since I'd arrived at Mouseford, I'd felt as if someone was watching me!
- The first clue is on page 43: I thought I'd seen Hans Ratson somewhere before, but where?
- On page 64, in the academy storeroom, someone was spying on us. Did you see him? Do you know whose paws they were?

A HORRIFIC HOWLING SOUND

I said good night to everyone and went to my room to get my rain slicker. Then I slipped off to the South Tower to get a breath of fresh **AIR**.

The rain and wind had eased up, but the storm was far from over.

My thoughts kept drifting back to **Violet** and the other four mouselings.

Even though Violet was very shy, I had a feeling that eventually those five mouselings would be friends.

I took a **deep** breath of cool night air. It was time for bed.

On my way back to my room, I passed in front of Hans

Ratson's door. **I COULD HEAR HIM SNORING.**

What an odd rodent he was! The more I thought about it, the more convinced I became that I had seen him somewhere before. But where?

I put the thought out of my head as I brushed my teeth and put on my favorite pajamas. Despite the ratnap I'd taken earlier, I was still worn out from my overnight trip to the island. I was *FAST ASLEEP* as soon as my head hit the pillow.

Hours later, at dawn, I woke with a start. The most horrific howling noise was echoing from outside my window. There was a terrible whoo-yooooo-olaaaaaaaaa sound.

And then the sound changed to wooo-whaaaaaaaaaaaaaaah-niooooooooo.

What in the name of stinky cheese could be making that dreadful noise?

THUNDER AND LIGHTNING

Every day, our planet experiences about 2,000 storms at one time with more than 100 lightning strikes per second. To calculate how far away the storm is, count the number of seconds between the lightning flash and the roar of thunder, then divide by five. For example, if you hear the thunder ten seconds after seeing a lightning flash, it means that the storm is about two miles away. Five seconds would be approximately one mile away.

THE GOOD-MORNING SERENADE!

Look out of the window,
Eyes of tender blue.
Look out of the window,
Down upon one who loves you!
My life without you
Is but a moldy rind of Swiss,
Look out of the window,
And blow me a kiss!

Thundering cattails! It was Vince Guymouse, that soggy **sewer rat**! He was flanked by two **familiar-looking** characters. By the looks of them, they were the third and fourth Whale brothers!

This really was too good a performance to

miss. I realized I'd have a better view from the WINDOW in the corridor. So I threw on a bathrobe and headed into the hallway.

Apparently, the *headmaster* had had the same idea. "It's the 'Good Morning Serenade,'" he explained. "It's an island tradition to sing and bring gifts to one's *beloved*. I wonder who the serenade is for."

At that moment, Nicky and Paulina peeked

Oilskin Whale

Vince Guymouse

Leopold Whale

out of their room. Violet, Pamela, and Colette were right behind them.

"It looks like *Mousey Sighs* has struck again!" Pamela said, giggling. "Vince is head over paws in love with Colette!"

Colette had the grace to blush.

In the meantime, Vince went on with his serenade:

Look out of the window, soft heart of Brie,
Or, if you prefer, come to the balcony.
Your smile is like a red, red rose,
My love just grows and grows!

At that moment, **Midge** and Boomer appeared beside us.

"Looks like he could use a little water," said Midge. "A nice cold bucket right in the snout would bring him back to his senses!"

Boomer gave her a dirty look. "I'd do the honors myself, dear sister, if only *someone* hadn't lost my garden hose!"

"Don't look at me!" Midge replied indignantly. "I haven't lost anything! **NOT A SINGLE, TEENSY, TINY THING!** And what about *you*? Do you know where my six cheese fondue pots have gone?"

Boomer shrugged. "How should I know? But while we're on the topic, what happened to my rake?"

As they bickered, Nicky **snapped** her fingers. "What do you say we go on a **RUN**?"

That sounded like a great idea to me. Exercise is my favorite way to start the day. We all agreed

Make a note of these three clues: a garden hose, six cheese fondue pots, and a rake. They'll be useful for solving the mystery!

except for Violet, who wanted to sleep a little more.

As I returned to my room to put on my tracksuit, I paused for a moment in front of Hans's room. Despite all the RACKET outside his window, he was still snoring. How bizarre!

My whiskers tingled. Something didn't seem right to me. I knocked on his door. ONCE, TWICE, THREE times.

I'm an investigative journalist, which means I'm a whisker more curious than your average mouse. Even so, I don't generally enter a room without being invited. But this time, I thought I smelled a rat.

WHATEVER HAPPENED TO HANS RATSON?

Imagine my surprise when I entered Hans's room and found it empty! The snoring I had heard from outside the door was nothing more than a **RECORDING**!

What had happened to Hans Ratson?

I scurried downstairs and went straight to the headmaster's office.

"What do you mean *DISAPPEARED*?" exclaimed the headmaster.

"I found this in his room," I explained as I showed him a mini stereo. "It was playing a CD of snoring **noises**."

"Someone put this recording in the room to make us think **HANS** was in his room **sleeping**," I explained. "But the truth is,

Zzzzzzzzzzzz!

he has **disappeared**!"

"THEA, I could really use your help with this matter," he said. His fur had gone white with worry. "We must find Hans Ratson at once! His parents will be sick with worry. And news of a missing student would be so harmful to Mouseford's reputation."

"Of course, I'll help," I promised. "I'll do whatever it takes."

I found a book!

Before I could finish my thought, **Boomer Whale** marched in. He looked pretty SERIOUS.

"Headmaster, I think one of the students has gone wandering down into the cellars! The door wasn't closed properly," he told us. "And I found a book belonging to Hans Ratson on the stairs."

Boomer held up the book to show us.

"Let's go look for him!" I said.

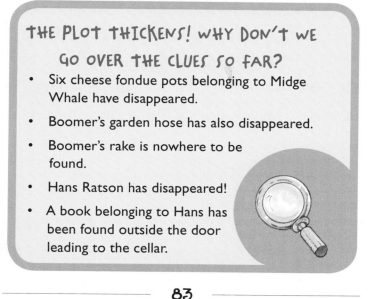

THE PLOT THICKENS! WHY DON'T WE GO OVER THE CLUES SO FAR?

- Six cheese fondue pots belonging to Midge Whale have disappeared.
- Boomer's garden hose has also disappeared.
- Boomer's rake is nowhere to be found.
- Hans Ratson has disappeared!
- A book belonging to Hans has been found outside the door leading to the cellar.

ANCIENT LEGENDS

"**Really?**" Nicky asked eagerly. "**WE GET TO GO DOWN TO THE CELLAR?**"

The mouselings were very excited. It hadn't been easy, but in the end the headmaster had agreed. I needed help solving this mystery, and my instincts told me these students were up for it. I'd promised the headmaster we'd all stay together.

"I know I can count on you not to **LET ME DOWN**, Thea!" Professor de Mousus told me. "We've got to find Hans as soon as possible."

"Don't worry, Headmaster!" exclaimed Pamela. "We can do this!"

Colette and Violet looked worried. "What's wrong, Colette?" Nicky teased.

"Afraid you'll **break a nail**?"

Colette stuck her tongue out at Nicky. "I don't have the right kind of clothes for this adventure. When I packed for Mouseford, I didn't expect I'd be going on underground expeditions!"

"Don't worry, you're perfect as you are," Pamela said.

Violet still looked a little doubtful. "Are you sure we won't get in trouble?"

Before I could respond, the headmaster appeared with Boomer, who was carrying a *FLASHLIGHT*. The mouselings all fell silent.

"Let's form a line with Boomer in the lead," I suggested. Everyone nodded, and we all lined up. Slowly, we started down a **DARK**, **dank** stairwell.

"I hope there aren't any spiders here!" Pamela said, shivering.

"Shhh!" scolded Boomer. "Stop squeaking and watch where you're going. It's very DANGEROUS!"

As we headed deeper underground, *Professor de Mousus* told us about the

The Vikings were great navigators.

They went in search of fertile lands.

frescoes that lined the walls. "These ancient pictures depict the legend of the beginnings of Mouseford Academy. According to tradition, the castle was built by the VIKINGS. They landed on this island, which they called **WHALE ISLAND**, more than a thousand years ago. They built their village around the island's largest natural spring. Today's island residents are the descendants of the Vikings."

After a few more minutes, we reached the bottom of the stairway.

when they landed on the island, they were surprised.

The land was more fertile than they had imagined, and

THE VIKINGS

No one really knows the origin of the word **Viking**. Some say it's from the old Norse word for pirate. Others say it's based on the Norse word for boy. From A.D. 800 to 1000, the Vikings sailed from northern Europe as far as North Africa. They were great navigators, and according to some scholars their *drakars*, or dragon-headed longboats, may have reached America long before **Christopher Columouse**!

Boomer shone the *FLASHLIGHT* on an ancient door decorated with STARS and **winged dragons**. High up on the wall, we could see Mouseford's motto carved into the stone:

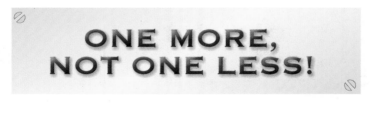

ONE MORE,
NOT ONE LESS!

THE DRAGON'S ROOM

The *headmaster* pulled out a large key ring. He selected a big brass key.

The door opened with a loud creak, and we stepped inside. I realized I was holding my breath in anticipation.

We were in a large, **rectangular** room with a high, vaulted ceiling. On the left, there was a huge stone fountain carved with five enormouse dragons. On the right, there was a statue of a huge, crouching winged dragon. I'm no 'fraidy mouse, but that statue made my tail curl.

"Welcome to the Dragon's Room," the headmaster said.

Boomer *LIT* a few

torches. As the light *GREW BRIGHTER*, we saw that the fountain's pool was full of water, which was spilling out of an **IRON** tap wrapped in a tube of green rubber.

"There's my hose!" exclaimed Boomer.

Behind the fountain, there was an inscription that was made of odd *SYMBOLS*

that looked like they belonged to some ancient language. The same symbols appeared on the cold stone floor.

"How peculiar," Violet murmured. "They look like letters, don't they?"

PAULINA pulled out her digital camera and started snapping photos.

I *smiled* at her enthusiasm.

INSCRIPTION BEHIND THE FOUNTAIN

"HEY, LOOK AT THAT!" Pamela piped up. She pointed to six *fondue pots* piled up in front of the dragon statue. "Aren't those Midge's pots?"

Clue

"They sure are!" exclaimed Boomer.

Colette took out a small *pink* notebook and started taking notes.

Meanwhile, Paulina made another discovery. "Look!" she cried. "There are wooden **splinters** on the floor!"

Boomer looked indignant. "There's the handle to my rake. It's completely ruined!" Then he looked around, puzzled. "So where's the rest of it?"

"And where is Hans Ratson?" the headmaster wondered.

"I have a hunch that the **KEY** to the whole mystery is this inscription," Paulina said.

"I think it's written in a **SECRET CODE.**"

"A **SECRET CODE**?" murmured Violet. "What can it mean?"

We stayed and looked around for a while longer, but no further clues came to light.

Finally, Professor de Mousus said it was time to go back

In the Dragon's Room, we found the hose, the six cheese fondue pots, and the broken rake. Note: The letters on the floor are the same as those in the inscription behind the dragon!

UPstairs. His brow was creased in worry. "I just wish we had more to go on," he said.

"Me, too," I replied.

"I was sure we'd find Hans in the cellar," the headmaster went on. "Where else could he be? According to legend, there are **SECRET** passageways from the Dragon's Room, but no one knows how to access them or where they lead. And they could be **DANGEROUS**."

I was too deep in thought to respond. There were a lot of clues, but they all seemed to point in different directions. I was looking forward to squeaking with my students about it. It would be good to get different perspectives on the case.

This photo taken by Violet shows the mysterious inscription in the Dragon's Room.

THERE'S A LITTLE TRUTH IN ALL LEGENDS

It had started to rain again. When I looked out the window, I saw Vince Guymouse's assistants carrying him away. He was still singing in that horribly off-key squeak of his:

"Look out of the window, my soft cheese spread,
Before the rain leaves me for dead!"

Pamela covered her ears with her paws. "Thank goodness they're leaving!"

Boomer hurried over to tell Midge we had found her fondue pots. But she didn't bother thanking him. She just started complaining — **FiRST**, because someone had taken them without asking, and **SECOND**, because they were covered with rust stains!

And that was before I told her she couldn't have them back until the investigation was over. She was OUTRAGED! "How will I cook dinner tonight?" she demanded.

"I'm sorry," I said firmly. "But I can't have my evidence covered with cheese fondue."

Midge stormed off in a huff.

The five mouselings and I gathered in my study to discuss our next steps.

PAULINA had no doubt. "Behind every legend there is an element of truth. There must be some connection between the legends of mice disappearing in the cellar and the disappearance of Hans Ratson."

Colette was a little more practical. "I think we should look at Hans Ratson's room. Maybe he left behind a clue."

"Nicky and I can go to the port to see if anyone has seen Hans," Pamela suggested. "I mean, we can't be sure that Hans is still here at Mouseford."

"Good point," said Colette. "While you're there, I'll look at his room."

"I can come with you," **Violet** suggested softly. It seemed like she was trying to break the ice a bit with Colette.

"I can come with you."

"Sure, that would be great," Colette replied with a smile.

In the meantime, Paulina turned on her **laptop**. I want to see if I can decipher the mysterious code we found in the Dragon's Room."

I sat down at my desk and smiled at my students. "I am so proud of you! Your instincts are excellent. Now, this is your **FIRST INVESTIGATION**, so remember:

Don't be fooled by appearances. Check out all the details, but never lose sight of the case as a whole. **And never be afraid to rethink your ideas.** If an idea doesn't seem to be leading you anywhere, maybe it's time to try a new idea! If you need help, I'm here whenever you want. But so far, you're off to a great start. I know you can do it!"

I am so proud of you!

WE HAVE UNTIL TOMORROW

I left the mouselings to their investigations. Then I went to Professor de Mousus's study to update him.

The professor ushered me in. "How is the weather out there, Thea?" he asked.

"Well, the **STORM** is almost over," I replied. "But that's not necessarily good news for our investigation. Once boats can travel to and from **WHALE ISLAND** again, it will be much more difficult to find Hans Ratson. We have until tomorrow, at the latest, before the harbor reopens."

The headmaster nodded gravely. "I called Hans's parents, but no one answered. They'll be so worried when they find out."

I was deep in thought. I gazed at the portraits on the wall around me as I reflected. One question haunted me: Why did I think I'd seen Hans Ratson before?

Meanwhile, *Professor de Mousus* was staring out the window. I felt sorry for him. He was such a wise, well-meaning rodent. He **cared** so deeply about the academy and its students. I knew he'd be crushed

if anything happened to Hans.

As we grow up, we often discover that the rodents we had always considered **BiG** and **STRONG** sometimes need help themselves. And even though we used to be so young and tiny, it's up to us to give them a helping paw.

I cleared my throat to get the headmaster's attention. "Professor de Mousus, why don't we take a *stroll* around the grounds? You taught me to do that. If you're feeling confused and you don't know what to do, take a nice long walk. It'll help clear your head."

The headmaster smiled at me. "That is an excellent suggestion, Thea," he said. "You are really looking out for me and for Mouseford. I am truly in your debt."

BEEP! BEEP! BEEP!

As I was talking with the headmaster, the mouselings continued their investigation. Paulina filled me in on everything that happened later. Colette and Violet had

returned from Hans Ratson's room, where they'd found some interesting clues.

"Look at this!" Colette told the others. "Look how many books he has on ancient codes!"

Violet already had her snout buried in one of the books and was reading *EAGERLY*.

Nicky and *Pamela* had returned, too, but they had no news. No one had seen Hans at the port. The storm had kept all the ships safe at home, and there had been no new arrivals on the island.

PAULINA looked up from her laptop. "I'm trying to figure out the key to the mysterious inscription in the *Dragon's Room*."

Suddenly, **Violet** squeaked loudly. "I've found something!"

She was waving some papers she had found in one of Hans Ratson's books. There was one sentence written over and over:

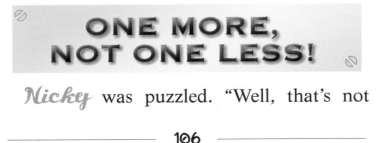

ONE MORE, NOT ONE LESS!

Nicky was puzzled. "Well, that's not

weird. It's the academy's motto."

Violet shook her snout. "But it's not just the school motto. Don't you remember? The sentence was also inscribed above the entrance to the Dragon's Room. I think it's an example of *ancient* writing — writing that's even older than the academy itself!"

There was a long silence. Then Paulina typed something into her computer, and it immediately started beeping.

Paulina stared at the screen for a minute. Then she squeaked, "I think **I'VE GOT IT**!"

Hurray!

Beep!
Beep!
Beep!

D IS FOR DRAGON!

One word had appeared on the screen: DRAGON!

"It worked!" Paulina exclaimed.

"But how?" asked Sam.

"I came up with a way to try to decipher the inscriptions," Paulina explained.

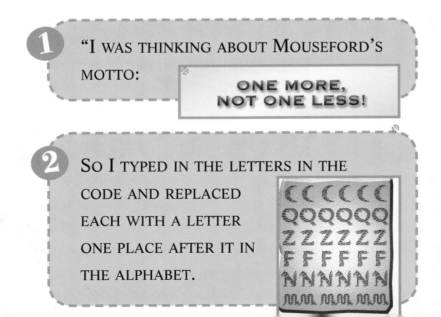

1 "I WAS THINKING ABOUT MOUSEFORD'S MOTTO:

ONE MORE, NOT ONE LESS!

2 SO I TYPED IN THE LETTERS IN THE CODE AND REPLACED EACH WITH A LETTER ONE PLACE AFTER IT IN THE ALPHABET.

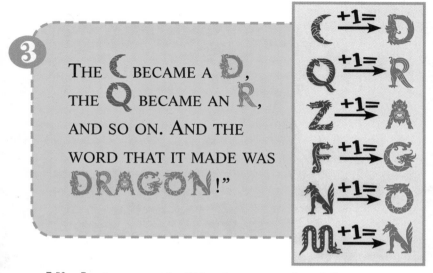

3 THE 𝐂 BECAME A 𝐃,
THE 𝐐 BECAME AN 𝐑,
AND SO ON. AND THE
WORD THAT IT MADE WAS
DRAGON!"

Violet gasped. "You're exactly right. One more, not one less!"

Pamela hugged Paulina. "**Way to go!**"

Only Colette was quiet. She watched the other mouselings celebrate for a minute, then pointed to the table, which was piled high with books, photos, and notes. "I don't mean to put mold on your cheese, but I think it's a bit too early to start celebrating. We still have **hundreds of mysteries** to solve!"

MIXV TFQE JB!
The heading above is a secret message! It is written in the Caesar cipher. This means letters are replaced by letters a certain distance ahead in the alphabet. This particular one is +3. So A = D, B = E, etc. Try deciphering the message. You can check your answer on page 114!

Colette was **right**: There were still lots of questions to be ANSWERED. My students all looked downcast for a moment.

"OK, mouselings," Paulina squeaked. "We know that to decipher the **MYSTERIOUS CODE**, we have to substitute one letter for another. So let's see what number works to **figure out** the message that's inscribed on the floor!"

They tried . . .

And tried . . .

And tried again.

But the words made no **sense**.

"There has to be a connection," said Violet.

"But what? what? **what?**" asked Nicky. She was getting frustrated.

The hours passed, and the mouselings were getting tired. In fact, they were all ready for a rat nap!

PAULINA was going cross-eyed from staring at the computer screen for too long. Pamela was pulling on her own fur in frustration. Nicky was fidgeting restlessly. Colette had shampooed her hair three times in hopes of getting inspiration.

Then, suddenly, it dawned on **Violet**. She took a deep breath.

"Back home in CHINA, we say that there comes a time when you should stand still instead of scurrying about and getting nowhere," Violet

A moment of inspiration...

told the others. "I think we've REACHED that moment."

And with that, she scampered out of the room.

Nicky stared after her. "What is she talking about?"

The other mouselings all shook their heads. They had no idea.

INVENT YOUR OWN SECRET CODE!

With the +3 code, "MIXV TFQE JB!" means "PLAY WITH ME!" If you go forward three letters in the alphabet, M becomes P, and so on.

Are you ready to invent your own secret code? Your code could be +2 or −1. (In the case of −1, you have to go back a letter. For example, for A, the letter you have to substitute is Z.) Use this system to write secret messages to all your friends!

THE BEGINNINGS OF A REAL TEAM

A few minutes later, Violet returned with a kettle of boiling water and her **red wooden box**. She opened it and took out a teapot and some very small china *cups*.

"This *tea set* belonged to my dear great-grandmother *Lotus Flower*," she told the other girls. "It is my most prized possession."

Violet crumbled a few dry leaves into the *teapot*.

"What's that?" Nicky asked curiously.

"It's *green tea*,"

answered Violet. "It gives you a big boost of **energy**. Plus, it tastes and smells delicious."

She was right. A moment later, the room was filled with a delicious-smelling aroma.

Pamela was especially interested in the **cheese** and **crystallized ginger** Violet was setting out on a tray. "That looks great!" she said. "I'm so hungry, I could eat a **whole elephant**!"

As soon as Violet was done setting everything out, the girls dug in. They'd worked up quite an appetite. There was total silence while they ate. Then, suddenly, they had the energy to think again.

"These letters on the floor are a real enigma," PAULINA mused. "They make no sense at all." She sat down at the **computer** to work at the letters again. All of a sudden, she *stopped* in her tiny tracks.

HABITS AND TRADITIONS

Green tea goes back a long, long way. According to legend, the first person to drink this tea was the Chinese emperor and herbalist Shen Nong Shi back in 2800 B.C. Tea has only been known to the Western World since the sixteenth century. Some say green tea keeps you young and healthy.

"Hang on, I think I've got something here!" she cried. The other mouselings gathered around her computer screen. "There are *twenty-six* letters, and they're all different. So maybe it's an **alphabet** of some kind. Of course! The letters on the floor don't hide a SECRET message of any kind. They make up a complete alphabet!"

Nicky was very excited about Paulina's discovery. "Thea was right. If an IDEA

doesn't seem to be leading you anywhere, maybe it's time to try a new one!'"

Pamela looked around her. She wanted another cup of tea. But every inch of the **TABLE** was covered with books and papers. So she placed her cup on one of Hans's books.

Violet was thinking aloud. "We've discovered that the letters on the floor correspond to an **alphabet**. But what use is that?"

"Maybe it's no use at all," Pamela replied as she poured the tea into her cup. The book,

which was balanced precariously on top of another book, started TOPPLING OVER AND OVER, AND OVER, AND OVER, AND OVER, AND OVER, AND OVER, AND OVER, AND OVER, AND OVER, AND OVER, AND OVER, AND OVER!

Violet looked up JUST IN TIME to see her great-grandmother's precious CUP about to smash into smithereens. "OH, NO!" she cried.

As quick as a kangaroo, Nicky GRABBED the cup. She caught it a second before it fell and broke!

At that moment, Violet's eyes LIT UP. "Chewy cheese bits, I've got it! Pamela, you're a genius!"

"Don't make fun of me!" exclaimed Pamela. "I'm sorry! I know I almost broke your cup, but it was an accident."

"Thank Nicky," said Violet. "If you'd BROKEN my cup, I would have been really upset! But I'm not making fun out of you, honestly I'm not. I've never been so serious in my life! Pamela, you really are a genius because you've cracked the case!"

THE DRAGON'S CODE

So what happened? When Violet saw the book about to topple under the weight of the cup, a thousand *LIGHTBULBS* switched on in her brain!

"There was a six-letter word inscribed on the wall behind the fountain in the Dragon's Room, right?" she said. "And there are six fondue pots, too. So I bet if we arrange the pots on the floor on top of the letters that make up the word DRAGON, and we fill them with water, something will happen."

"That is absolutely brilliant!" Pamela squeaked.

"Come on!" cried Nicky.

"Let's go!"

The **MOUSELINGS** grabbed a few FLASHLIGHTS and hastily scrawled me a **note** that said they were going down to the Dragon's Room. They stopped in the dining hall, where they borrowed a few of Midge's fondue pots for their EXPERIMENT.

As quiet as mice, the students scampered down to the cellars. As soon as they got to the Dragon's Room, they placed the pots on top of the letters that

spelled DRAGON. Then they hooked up the hose.

They filled the pots on top of the letters D, R, A, G, and O.

Nothing happened. **Not a thing!**

When they started filling the pot on letter N, they all held their breath.

PAULINA was feeling *really anxious*. "What if something scary happens once we fill that pot? What if the roof collapses?"

At that precise moment, Pamela finished filling the last pot.

For a moment, nothing happened. Then the floor started *vibrating*.

"Jumping tuna fish!" Colette shrieked. The mouselings **grabbed** one another and held on tight. They watched the six **stone** slabs under the pots.

As they watched, the slabs slowly began to *sink into the floor*. They sank so far down, the pots almost disappeared from view!

"**Now what?**" breathed Colette.

As if to answer her, the enormouse stone dragon's mouth suddenly opened: **CRACK!**

Pamela leaped up. "**WOW!**" she shouted. "**IT'S A SECRET PASSAGEWAY!**" She was about to run right in when Nicky grabbed her paw.

A SECRET PASSAGEWAY!

"Wait!" Nicky cried. "Hang on a minute."

Pamela didn't understand. "Oh, do you want to go first?"

Nicky laughed and shook her snout. "NO! I just think we should look before we leap!"

They all took a look. Inside the DRAGON's mouth was Boomer's rake, *broken cleanly in half*.

Nicky gazed at the dragon's mouth. "It reminds me of the crocodiles back home." She took off her hat. "In Australia, everyone knows you have to be very careful with crocodiles."

And with that, she took careful aim and threw her hat directly into the mouth of the dragon. A moment later, its massive jaws snapped shut: **SNAP!**

At the same time, the six stone slabs sunk in the floor **SHOT UP**, *HURLING* the six pots

against the ceiling.

"Cover up, quick!!!" shouted Pamela. "It's a booby trap!"

All five mouslings huddled together, covering their snouts with their paws. The pots bounced off the ceiling and hit the floor, making a tremendous racket. The water put out all the torch flames. Everything went **PiTCH-BLACK**.

WHO KNOWS IF THERE ARE OTHER TRAPS?

Nicky reached for her *FLASHLIGHT* and turned it on. Its thin beam lit up the room.

"Paulina? Pamela? Colette? **Violet?**" she called. "Where are you?"

One after the other, Pamela, Violet, Colette, and Paulina EMERGED from the darkness. Everyone was safe and sound. But they were all DRENCHED from the tips of their tails to the tips of their whiskers.

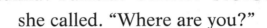

"Let's open the dragon's mouth again!" proposed *Pamela*.

"You sure don't give up!" said Paulina, laughing.

So the five mouslings arranged the pots on top of the letters D-R-A-G-O-N, filled them with WATER, and again the dragon opened its mouth.

"What do we do now?" asked Colette.

"Someone tried to KEEP the dragon's mouth open using Boomer's rake, but it didn't work," said Pamela. "The rake broke, but we can do better." She rummaged around in her bag, pulling out an enormouse WRENCH. "Unlike the rake, this won't break!"

The others were taken aback.

"Do you always go around with one of those things in your bag?" Violet asked.

"Of course!" said Pamela. She seemed surprised by the other students' reaction. "I've got a whole collection of them. You never know when you'll come across an ENGINE that needs to be repaired!"

Pamela and Nicky quickly propped up the wrench between the teeth of the **DRAGON**. It was perfect for holding the dragon's mouth open. There was just

enough space for the mouselings to squeeze through.

"I wonder if there are any other booby traps," Nicky muttered.

Violet looked a little scared. "I sure hope not!"

WE'RE ALMOST AT THE END OF THE MYSTERY. WHAT PURPOSE DID ALL THE CLUES SERVE?

- The hose filled the fondue pots with water.
- The six cheese pots set off the mechanism that opened the stone dragon's mouth.
- The rake held the dragon's mouth open.

BUT WE STILL NEED TO FIGURE OUT WHERE HANS RATSON IS!

AAAHHHHH! SPLASH!

Nervously, the five students crept inside the **stone** dragon's mouth.

Inside, there was a staircase that led down. The mouselings began their descent, carefully placing one paw after another.

Colette stopped to reapply her *pink* lipstick when Nicky put her paw down on the **THiRD Step**. There was a loud **CLICK**! Before any of the students could react, the stairs all turned downward and the staircase became a **slide**!

Colette tried to hang on, but all she managed to do was leave a really long *pink* smear on the wall with her lipstick.

The mouselings fell **DOOOOOOOWN!!!!**
"**AAAAHHHHHHHH!**" they all shrieked.

Until . . .

SPLASH!

At last, they landed in a dark underground river. They were in the **sewers** of Mouseford Castle!

"Is **everyone** OK?" shouted Paulina.

"Is everybody with us?" cried Nicky.

"I'm **wet**, but I'm here," Pamela answered.

"Me, too!" said Violet.

"I'm here, too," said Colette.

"I think we're caught in some kind of *current*," Nicky said. "Do you feel it?"

Aaaaahhhhh!!!

Violet searched about frantically for Frilly. "Frilly? Oh, where has he gone?"

"I see him!" said Nicky. "There he is!"

Sure enough, Frilly's **pumpkin house** was bobbing dangerously in the water. The cricket was about to drown!

Colette was closest. "I'll get him!" With two quick strokes, she reached the pumpkin. But then she was unable to swim back to her friends. "The *current* is too strong!"

PAULINA reached out her paw. "Here, hang on to me!"

Nicky was closest to Paulina. "And you hold on to me!"

Pamela grabbed Nicky. Soon all five mouselings were holding on to one another.

"Hey! I've found land again!" **Violet** called. She pulled herself out of the water and reached out to Pamela. "Grab my paw!"

AAAHHHHH! SPLASH!

Pamela grabbed it.

"*Frilly!* Come here!" Violet shouted.

The cricket popped his head out of the pumpkin house. Then he jumped onto Colette's arm, then onto Paulina's head, then onto Nicky's hat, and finally right onto the tip of Pamela's snout.

"GET HIM OFF MEEEEEEEEEE!"

Pamela stared at the cricket for a moment in shock. Then she SHRIEKED.

Frilly seemed just as scared as Pamela was! He quickly jumped into Violet's waiting paws. He was safe at last!

One after the other, the mouselings pulled themselves out of the water.

Violet hugged each of her friends in turn. She held on to Pamela for an especially **long** time. "Thank you," she whispered.

Nicky sniffed. "Eww. Do you smell that?"

Colette giggled. "Yeah. I think it's us."

Suddenly, their laughter was interrupted by a piercing cry.

HEEEEEEEEEELP!!!

YOU KNOW, I THINK I RECOGNIZE HIM!

"What was that?" **Violet** whispered.

"Maybe it's Hans!" PAULINA said.

"Let's find out!" said *Nicky*.

"I see a light over there," said *Colette*.

"Let's check it out," said *Pamela*.

So the mouselings followed Colette into the light. A few moments later, they found themselves in a huge **cave** lit by rays of **sunshine** that filtered down through a few cracks in the ceiling. The floors were **covered** in sewer water.

But what really got the students' attention were the remains of an enormouse **VIKING** ship! Its **PROW** was in the shape of a magnificent dragon's head. Next to it was

a strange contraption built with cables, wheels, and **GEARS**. And someone was hanging upside-down.

"**HANS RATSON?**" asked Paulina.

"It looks like him," spluttered Violet. "But it isn't Hans Ratson!"

Whoever he was, he was happy to see them. "**I beg you, please help me!**"

Impulsive Pamela was already running toward him. The other mouselings hung behind cautiously. They weren't sure what to make of the scene.

Suddenly, Colette **SHRIEKED**, "Look! There on the ground! It's Hans Ratson's hair! That monster has **plucked** out all his hair!"

Paulina laughed. "Don't be silly, Colette! It's just a **WIG**."

Whoever it was shouted, "Well then? Are you going to get me down or not?"

That was the cue for me and Professor de Mousus to burst onto the scene. We'd found the note the mouselings had left me and followed in their pawsteps to the sewers.

Who? Me?

Violet was the first to see us. "MS. STILTON! Professor! You're here!'

"Thanks to you!" I said, smiling. "And, Colette, thank *you* for letting me know there was a trap on the third step of the staircase."

"Who? Me?" said Colette.

"Yes, I found the *pink* smear you left with your lipstick," I said. "It was ingenious!"

Colette blushed. "Um, well, it wasn't exactly planned," she murmered. "I was slipping down and — anyway,

I'm glad it helped!"

WHO IS THAT HANGING UPSIDE DOWN?

"Well, Professor Stilton?" Nicky asked. "Do you know who that is hanging upside DOWN?"

"Yes, I think so," I replied. "Do you know Bartholomew Sparkle? He's a journalism teacher, and his PHOTO is hanging in the headmaster's study. He disguised himself with a WIG and thick GLASSES, transforming himself into Hans Ratson!"

"That's right!" **Violet** agreed. "I saw his picture in the headmaster's study, too!"

As we were talking, Professor de Mousus was busy freeing Hans Ratson (a.k.a. Bartholomew Sparkle). Professor Sparkle rubbed the place on his ankle where the rope had been, then limped over to us. "Well, hello there! Were you talking about me?"

WE ALL BURST OUT LAUGHING.

What a strange situation!

"Professor Sparkle, you have a lot of EXPLAINING to do," I said. "Tell me something: Were you spying on

BARTHOLOMEW SPARKLE **IS** IS HANS RATSON.

me from MOUSEFORD ACADEMY when I landed?"

He spread out his paws. "Professor Stilton, '**SPIED**' isn't quite the word I'd use. Let's just say I was CURIOUS to see what you were like. When I was a student, the headmaster always **referred** to you as a model student, so I wanted to check you out."

My fur turned a little pink, I must admit. I was extremely FLATTERED.

A DIFFICULT DECISION

"I think it's time for me to come clean," Professor Sparkle **said**. "Back when I was still a student at Mouseford, I found a book called *Booby Traps: A Beginner's Guide* in the library. It was about the cellars in Mouseford Academy. So I decided to **explore** them. Once I was inside the **Dragon's Room**, I managed to decipher the code with some help from the book I'd found in the library," Professor Sparkle explained. "I went back up

A SHORT SUMMARY OF ALL THE CLUES!

THE FONDUE + THE DRAGON

to the dining hall and grabbed a few fondue pots from Midge's kitchen. Then I filled them up and used Boomer's rake to **BLOCK** the mouth of the stone dragon."

"When the dragon's mouth closed, it broke the rake. After being *carried along* by the sewer currents, I ended up in a Viking trap, which is where you found me."

"But why did you disguise yourself as HANS RATSON?" I asked.

"Because I wanted to make sure I could explore the cellars undisturbed," Professor Sparkle said sheepishly. "Luckily, you arrived and saved the day, otherwise I might have been hanging there for years!"

"Well, I can't say I approve of your methods,

THE HOSE

THE RAKE + THE WIG

Bartholomew," the *headmaster* said. "But what an amazing discovery! We'll have to get a team of archaeologists down here."

Together, we all headed back upstairs.

An hour later, the headmaster called me to his office. "Thea, do you think the *mouselings* deserve some kind of punishment?"

I reflected for a moment. "They went down to the cellars without asking for permission, and that was **WRONG**. But they did rescue Professor Sparkle."

The *headmaster* nodded. "Will you go ask them to join me in the Great Hall, Thea?" he asked.

"Of course!" I said. I scampered away to the

students' dorm rooms. When I arrived, they were all very worried.

"Will we be expelled?" asked PAULINA.

"It's all my fault!" exclaimed Nicky.

Colette shook her snout. "That's not true. We were all in agreement."

"We're all responsible!" **Violet** declared.

When we entered the Great Hall, there were loads of students and teachers there, too.

Someone in the back started clapping. Then another mouse, and then another.

What a fabumouse surprise!

The headmaster had prepared a very special "punishment!"

"Colette, PAULINA, Pamela,

Violet, and *Nickey*, we owe you many thanks for finding Professor Sparkle and for discovering the secret that has been hidden below Mouseford Academy! Your first assignment in Professor Stilton's adventure journalism class is to write a detailed account of this adventure."

I was so relieved that the mouselings were going to stay. Maybe my students could even help me write a book! I already had the title all picked out: The Dragon's Code!

MORE THAN FRIENDS: SISTERS!

Of course, there were still a few details to sort out.

"What about my RAKE, my dear Professor Sparkle?" asked Boomer Whale.

"And what about my six **fondue pots**?" asked Midge Whale.

"And what about the *receipt* for that letter I gave you?" asked Mercury the postman. "Please tell me where it is, Ms. Stilton."

Yes, he was back on Whale Island. The **THREE** Whale siblings were together now, and holey cheese, they were triple trouble!

Professor Sparkle promised to buy a new rake for Boomer.

The *mouselings* promised to polish

Midge's fondue pots until they shone.

As for me, I gave Mercury my BRIGHTEST smile. "I heard that you came all the way to New Mouse City just to bring me Professor de Mousus's invitation," I told him.

"Of course! What else would I have done, put it in the mail?" he snorted.

I batted my eyelashes at him and kissed him on the cheek. "Thanks a million!"

At that, he turned as red as the wrapper on a wheel of Gouda.

The Whales all headed off to their various tasks. Soon I was left with the five new best friends, who were hugging one another.

I looked at them and smiled. These five mouselings were all so different from one another. Each had different PERSONALITIES, *PASSIONS*, flaws, and *dreams*. Working together taught them that being different can be a huge **advantage**! Different perspectives give everyone a chance to learn something.

"So are we all friends now?" **Violet** whispered.

Colette smiled.

PAULINA gave her a hug.

Nicky put her hat on.

"We're more than friends!" said Pamela. "We're sisters!"

THEA SISTERS

Want to read the next adventure
of the Thea Sisters?
I can't wait to tell you all about it!

THEA STILTON AND THE MOUNTAIN OF FIRE

The Thea Sisters head to Australia to help solve a mystery on Nicky's family's small farm. It turns out that a flock of sheep is losing all its wool. The friends set off on a tour of Australia to search for a cure to the sheep's ailment. Of course, there are tons of obstacles in their way, and the mouselings must first climb over mountains, survive a flood, and avoid the traps of an invisible enemy! It's an adventure Down Under that they're sure to remember forever!

And don't miss any of our other fabumouse adventures!

#ST TREASURE OF THE MERALD EYE

#2 THE CURSE OF THE CHEESE PYRAMID

#3 CAT AND MOUSE IN A HAUNTED HOUSE

#4 I'M TOO FOND OF MY FUR!

FOUR MICE EEP IN THE JUNGLE

#6 PAWS OFF, CHEDDARFACE!

#7 RED PIZZAS FOR A BLUE COUNT

#8 ATTACK OF THE BANDIT CATS

FABUMOUSE CATION FOR ERONIMO

#10 ALL BECAUSE OF A CUP OF COFFEE

#11 IT'S HALLOWEEN, YOU 'FRAIDY MOUSE!

#12 MERRY CHRISTMAS, GERONIMO!

#13 THE PHANTOM OF THE SUBWAY

#14 THE TEMPLE OF THE RUBY OF FIRE

#15 THE MONA MOUSA CODE

#16 A CHEESE-COLORED CAMPER

#17 WATCH YOUR WHISKERS, STILTON!

#18 SHIPWRECK ON THE PIRATE ISLANDS

#19 MY NAME IS STILTON, GERONIMO STILTON

#20 SURF'S UP, GERONIMO!

#21 THE WILD, WILD WEST

#22 THE SECRET OF CACKLEFUR CASTLE

A CHRISTMAS TALE

#23 VALENTINE'S DAY DISASTER

#24 FIELD TRIP TO NIAGARA FALLS

#25 THE SEARCH FOR SUNKEN TREASURE

#26 THE MUMMY WITH NO NAME

#27 THE CHRISTMAS TOY FACTORY

#28 WEDDING CRASHER

#29 DOWN AND OUT DOWN UNDER

#30 THE MOUSE ISLAND MARATHON

#31 THE MYSTERIOUS CHEESE THIEF

CHRISTMAS CATASTROPHE

#32 VALLEY OF THE GIANT SKELETONS

#33 GERONIMO AND THE GOLD MEDAL MYSTERY

#34 GERONIMO STILTON, SECRET AGENT

35 A VERY RY CHRISTMAS

#36 GERONIMO'S VALENTINE

#37 THE RACE ACROSS AMERICA

THEA STILTON AND THE DRAGON'S CODE

And don't forget to look for

THEA STILTON AND THE MOUNTAIN OF FIRE

#38 A FABUMOUSE SCHOOL ADVENTURE

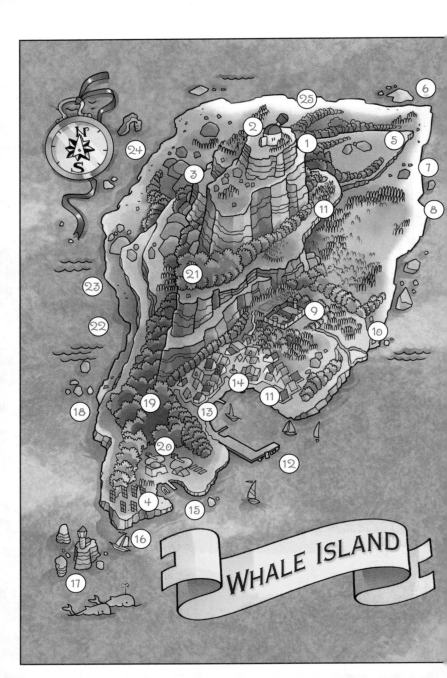

WHALE ISLAND

MAP OF WHALE ISLAND

1. Falcon Peak
2. Observatory
3. Mount Landslide
4. Solar Energy Plant
5. Ram Plain
6. Very Windy Point
7. Turtle Beach
8. Beachy Beach
9. Mouseford Academy
10. Kneecap River
11. Mariner's Inn
12. Port
13. Squid House
14. Town Square
15. Butterfly Bay
16. Mussel Point
17. Lighthouse Cliff
18. Pelican Cliff
19. Nightingale Woods
20. Marine Biology Lab
21. Hawk Woods
22. Windy Grotto
23. Seal Grotto
24. Seagulls Bay
25. Seashell Beach

THANKS FOR READING,
AND GOOD-BYE UNTIL OUR
NEXT ADVENTURE!

THEA SISTERS